Banana Beer

Carol Carrick
Pictures by Margot Apple

ALBERT WHITMAN & COMPANY • MORTON GROVE, ILLINOIS

The text typeface is Bembo.
The illustrations were done in watercolor and pencil.

Library of Congress Cataloging-in-Publication Data
Carrick, Carol.
Banana beer / Carol Carrick; illustrated by Margot Apple.
p.   cm.
Summary: Charlie the orangutan's life is adversely affected
by his father's addiction.
ISBN 0-8075-0568-4
[1. Orangutan—Fiction. 2. Alcoholism—Fiction.]
I. Apple, Margot, ill. II. Title.
PZ7.C2344Ban 1995   94-256
[E]—dc20   CIP
                                                              AC

Charlie sat on the porch waiting for his dad. They liked to rock in the hammock together and tell funny stories.

But when his dad came home, he gave Charlie lots of wet kisses that smelled like banana beer, as usual. And when he poured himself some more beer at dinnertime, he knocked over the glass.

"You've had enough," said Charlie's mom.

"No one tells *me* what to do in my own house," said his dad.

"It was an accident," said Charlie.

But no one heard him because his mom and dad were shouting. This always happened when his dad drank too much.

Charlie didn't feel like eating now.

The next day his dad was in a sorry mood. So Charlie asked him, "Please don't drink anymore."

And his dad nodded and said, "Okay." But it wasn't the first time he had promised.

His dad did stop, but not for very long. Saturday night Charlie's mom and dad were drinking with their friends. It was hard for Charlie to sleep when they got really noisy. Even the neighbors yelled, "Quiet down!" and threw coconuts at them.

The next morning his parents slept late, and there was nothing for breakfast, so Charlie ate the chips that were in a bowl on the table. He even tried the banana beer that somebody had left in a glass.

"Ugghh!" He thought it was awful.

Later that day, when his dad came outside, Charlie was playing with his friend Ruby.

"Let's see those marbles," said his dad.

"But I was just getting ready to shoot," said Charlie.

"I used to be pretty good at marbles," said his dad. He aimed at Ruby's marble and missed. Then he aimed again and again, and he missed every time. When his dad tried to stand up he fell over, almost on top of Ruby, and the marbles scattered.

Charlie's mother came to the door. "Those children were playing nicely," she said. "Why don't you leave them alone."

"You keep out of this," said his dad. "We're having fun."

But Charlie wasn't having fun. Neither was Ruby. "Let's not play here anymore," she said. And from then on, they played at her house.

Soon Charlie's dad was late every night, and when he came home, he smelled like banana beer. Some mornings he didn't get up for work. Charlie's mom had to call the boss and say his dad was sick. This made her angry. She seemed angry with Charlie, too. "Pick up your junk," she said. "Don't leave it for me to do."

His mom didn't usually talk to him like that.

And one day his dad stumbled over Charlie's favorite truck and broke it. "It's your fault," he said. "You shouldn't leave it in the way."

Maybe it *was* my fault, thought Charlie. Maybe everything's my fault. Maybe Dad wouldn't drink so much if I was a better boy.

So Charlie tried to be quiet when his dad was home sleeping. He picked up his toys and took baths without anyone asking him to.

Still Charlie's dad went on drinking. After his mom
kissed Charlie goodnight, she waited up. Charlie heard them
argue when his dad came home. He almost wished, now,
that his dad would stay away. It was nicer without him.

But Charlie was happy at school. When he worked hard, his teacher, Miss Lovewell, put a star on his workbook. "Good job," she said, and Charlie felt proud.

One day Miss Lovewell told the class to put their workbooks away. She passed out paper and crayons. "I want each of you to make a wish," she said.

Doris sat next to Charlie. "I want a pony," she hollered. "One with a long mane and tail."

"Don't tell me your wish," said Miss Lovewell. "I want you to make a picture of it."

Charlie thought about what he would draw.

Maybe he would draw a red truck like the one his dad had broken. Or maybe he would draw himself swimming. His dad always promised to take him to the beach, but he never did.

Charlie thought about how his mom and dad were fighting all the time. He made angry marks on the paper and pressed so hard that his crayon broke. Charlie crushed the paper into a ball and threw it on the floor.

"That's not what you're supposed to do with your paper," said Doris.

"Nosey!" said Charlie. "Mind your own business." He said it in such a loud voice that the other children turned to stare at him.

"You mind your own business, too!" Charlie yelled at them all. Then he ran to the bathroom and slammed the door.

Charlie thought Miss Lovewell would make him come out. He sat on the toilet seat till the rest of the children went home, but no one came to get him.

Charlie peeked out the door to see if Miss Lovewell
was angry.

She called him over to her desk. "Sometimes it helps to
talk to a grown-up friend," she said, putting her arm around
him. "Someone who cares about you." When she said that,
Charlie felt like crying.

Miss Lovewell had a nice lap. Charlie would have liked to
sit on it. Instead he told her about his dad. "If he loved me,"
Charlie said, "he wouldn't be so angry all the time."

"Your dad isn't angry with *you*," said Miss Lovewell.
"That's how banana beer makes him feel."

"But if he loved me he would stop drinking it," said
Charlie.

"Your dad does love you," Miss Lovewell said. "And I bet
he *has* tried to stop drinking, many, many times. That's why
he is angry—with himself."

That afternoon Charlie played at Ruby's house.

"Mmmm," said Charlie. "The kitchen smells good."

So Ruby's mom invited him for dinner. Charlie folded the napkins, and Ruby set the table.

When Ruby's dad came home, he had a big shopping bag.

"What did you bring?" Ruby asked.

Her daddy gave her a big hug. "Something for everyone," he said. The bag was full of coconuts.

During dinner, Ruby's little sister spilled her milk, but nobody yelled at her. Charlie liked eating here. He wished he never had to leave.

When it was late, Charlie's dad came to take him home.
"Did you have a good time?" he asked.

Charlie nodded.

His dad squeezed Charlie's hand. "I'm glad about that,"
he said, but his face looked sad all the same.

Charlie could see that his dad loved him. He had felt it
in the way he squeezed his hand.

The next day when Charlie went to school, he drew a wish on his paper. In the wish he was swinging on the porch with his dad. And they were telling each other stories the way they used to, and they were laughing.

Charlie is not alone. One out of every four families has a problem with alcohol or drugs. Charlie and his mom might feel happier and stronger if they joined a group like Al-Anon where they could talk about their feelings. And, maybe someday, Charlie's dad will get help for himself.